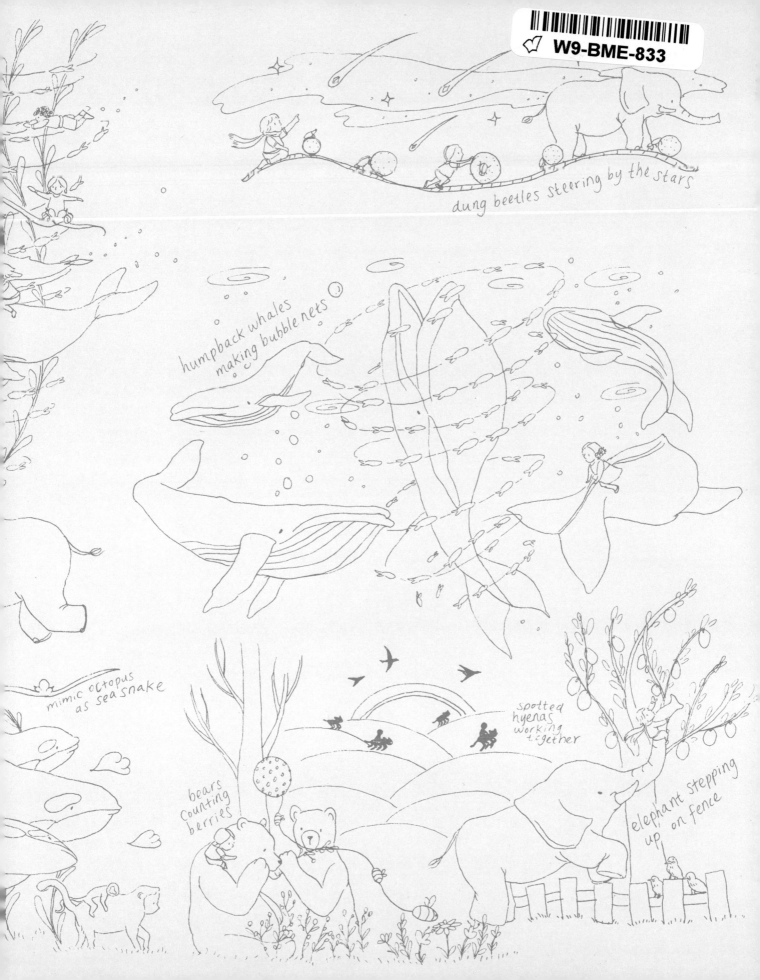

dung beetles steering by the stars

humpback whales making bubble nets

mimic octopus as sea snake

bears counting berries

spotted hyenas working together

elephant stepping up on fence

Wild Ideas

For Cookie Dough and Esmé, with gratitude for showing me the incredible opportunities that come from being entirely wrong—E.K.

To my loving dad, Sooyeon, my personal art critic and mom, Eunyoung, and my little brother, Jungmin.
Great thanks to Elin Kelsey and Mary Beth for giving me the opportunity to create the art for this book, and to everyone who worked together to let the magic happen—S.K.

Owlkids Books acknowledges the financial support of the Canada Council for the Arts, the Ontario Arts Council, the Government of Canada through the Canada Book Fund (CBF) and the Government of Ontario through the Ontario Media Development Corporation's Book Initiative for our publishing activities.

Published in Canada by
Owlkids Books Inc.
10 Lower Spadina Avenue
Toronto, ON M5V 2Z2

Published in the United States by
Owlkids Books Inc.
1700 Fourth Street
Berkeley, CA 94710

Library and Archives Canada Cataloguing in Publication

Kelsey, Elin, author
        Wild ideas / written by Elin Kelsey ; illustrated by Soyeon Kim.

ISBN 978-1-77147-062-9 (bound)

        1. Problem solving--Juvenile literature. I. Kim, Soyeon, illustrator II. Title.

BF449.K44 2015   j153.4'3   C2014-906145-5

Library of Congress Control Number: 2014947497

The artwork in this book was rendered as dioramas.
The text is set in Frutiger.
Edited by: Mary Beth Leatherdale
Designed by: Barb Kelly
Photographed by: Michael Cullen, TPG Digital Art Services

Manufactured in Shenzhen, Guangdong, China, in November 2014, by WKT Co. Ltd.
Job #14CB1113

A   B   C   D   E   F

 Publisher of Chirp, chickaDEE and OWL
www.owlkidsbooks.com

Wild Ideas

Elin Kelsey

Artwork by Soyeon Kim

Owlkids Books

Problems are like sticker burrs.
They **poke**.
They **prick**.
They **nag**.

But sometimes,
problems spark marvelous ideas.

zzzip!

Step outside.
Look.
If squirrels can learn to cross roads
by watching people,
what can you learn by watching squirrels?

All around you, creatures seek solutions.
Pigeons procrastinate.
Bees calculate.
Elephants innovate.
Bears keep count.

When orangutans feel puzzled,
they stop and think.

They plan.

They weave safe places to rest.

Lots of problems require you to hold tight.
But not all of them.

Sometimes *you **just need to**...*

Le*ap!*

Make like a gibbon
and throw yourself into
a new situation.

When these animals want to
make something happen…
they try.

They get frustrated.

They try again.

They invent tools.

Chimpanzees fold leaves to spoon
cool drinks of water.

Sea otters balance rocks on their
bellies, perfect for cracking crabs.

A dozen humpback whales blow
a fine net of bubbles to trap tasty fish.
Pop!
Pop!
POP!
GULP!

Like you, the mimic octopus is
a master of make believe.
Is that a deadly sea snake?
A harmless flatfish?

A poisonous lionfish parading
its venom-tipped spines?

You turn to friends and family
for support, and so do other animals.
Ravens use gestures to offer ideas.
Hyenas cooperate to help the hunt.

Killer whales rely on their mothers' wisdom.

Baboons get guidance from their dads.

And when they're seeking direction,
dung beetles look to the heavens
and steer by the Milky Way.

Problems that need solving
will always be part of life.

Untame your imagination...

A world of wild ideas awaits.